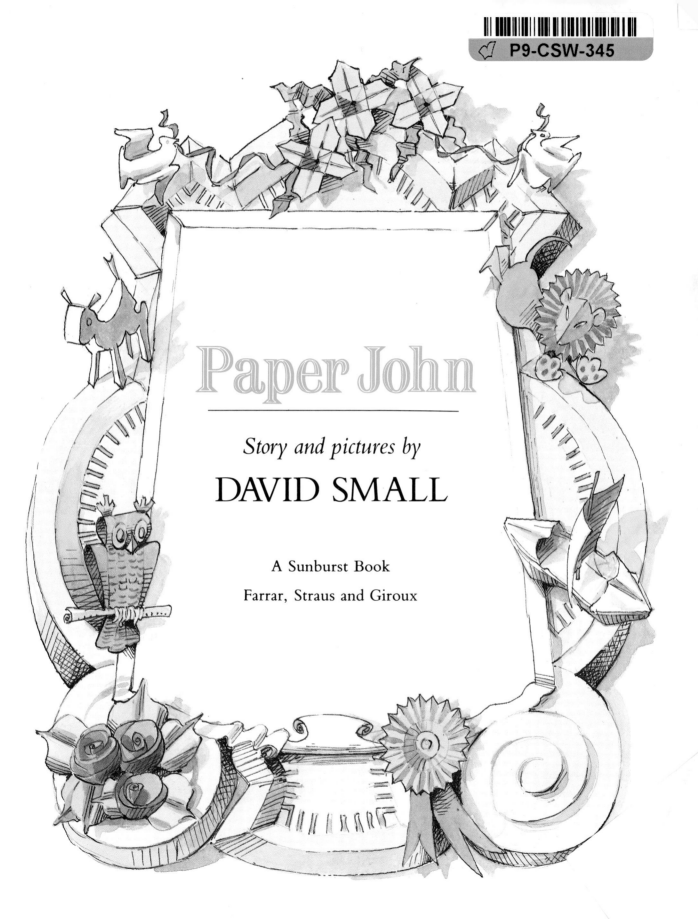

Paper John

Story and pictures by

DAVID SMALL

A Sunburst Book

Farrar, Straus and Giroux

To Sherry

A stranger wearing a paper hat came into a town at the edge of the sea. He stopped on a busy corner and took some paper from his pocket. Bending, scoring, pinching, he made a perfect rose.

Soon the stranger, whose name was John, had made an armful of paper flowers, and a woman bought the bouquet.

John built a paper house for himself down by the sea, and he lacquered the walls just as the Chinese do their paper umbrellas, to keep the rain from soaking through. Inside, it was cozy and warm.

He hung fishing poles out the window and caught his dinner fresh from the sea.

Children came from all over town to meet the man who lived in a paper house. He folded boats for every child and they had a grand regatta.

The townsfolk saw that he was gentle and good-natured, and he became known as Paper John. It was said he could get along with the devil himself. And, as it happened, he soon had the chance.

One night, Paper John was making a kite, round and golden like the sun. He was just finishing when his fishing poles began to bob as if he had caught an enormous fish. Then he heard a voice outside mumbling, muttering, and cursing.

Paper John went to the window. Looking down, he saw a little man tangled in the fishing lines. The more the man struggled, the tighter he was bound. Quickly, Paper John pulled him up into the house and freed him from the lines.

The little man was completely gray. His eyes and his clothes and skin were gray, and he had scraggly gray teeth. He was, in fact, a devil making his evil way through the world. He lived by taking whatever he could get for nothing. He was such a poor devil that he had only one devilish trick to play: he could command the four winds. However, since he could do this trick just once, he was saving it for when he really needed it.

As soon as he was set free of the lines, he cried in a whining voice, "I'm hungry!"

"Hungry? Why then, you shall eat!" exclaimed Paper John.

"Where shall I sit?" the devil demanded.

"Sit here," said Paper John, quickly making a seat and a table, on which he served a supper of bread, cheese, and fish.

The devil ate greedily, then yawned. "I'm tired," he announced. "Where shall I sleep?"

Paper John folded a bed. The devil fell onto it and immediately began to snore.

Paper John finished making the golden kite, then climbed into his own bed and tried to sleep. But the devil's snores kept him awake and he stayed up most of the night folding paper sheep to pass the time.

The next day was market day. As usual, Paper John carried
his goods to the public square to sell them. The devil followed
along behind him and, as they reached the square, he min-
gled with the crowd.

Suddenly, cries of "THIEF!" rang out as people discovered their pockets had been picked. The devil scurried out of the marketplace like a gray rat. Seeing him running away, Paper John wondered, "Why is that little fellow in such a hurry?"

On his way out of town, the devil passed by Paper John's house. He remembered the golden kite and said to himself, "I can escape just like a bird!"

He stole the kite, ran to the church, and sneaked up the bell tower. Then he climbed to the very tip of the spire.

The first breeze that came along blew the kite aloft. Paper John was astonished to see his golden kite flying high over the rooftops. Then he noticed the little gray man hanging on behind.

As the kite was tossed up and down by the breeze, a gold watch and a wallet shook loose from the devil's brimming pockets. When they fell to the street, Paper John knew that the devil was the thief.

Quickly, he made a paper falcon with a sharp beak and flung it into the air. It struck the kite, and the devil plummeted toward the earth, where the police were waiting to take him to jail.

Sitting alone in the dark jail cell, the devil reckoned that the time had come to use his one trick. He called the four winds together with magic words. The winds came, and blew a hole in the jailhouse wall.

They stood before the little gray man, awaiting his command.

"Destroy the town!" the devil cried. "Blow it all into the sea, especially Paper John and his flimsy house!"

The sky grew black and the four winds howled like demons as they ripped and roared from one end of town to the other.

Out in the churning water, people clung to their rooftops and other debris, praying that they would not drown. Then, high in the air, along came Paper John's house.

Paper John was taking a nap when the house was lifted off the ground.

As the house tumbled through the air, Paper John and all his paper things were tossed about. Then the house splashed into the water.

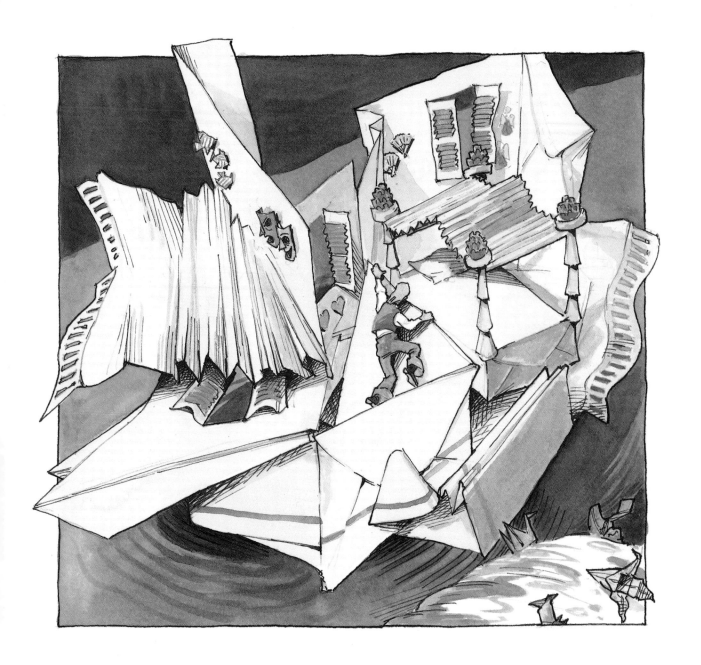

Paper John saw there was only one thing to do. He set to work, bending, scoring, pinching as fast as he could.

The walls of the house began to change shape. At first, it looked like a giant flower unfolding.

Then like a giant bird.

Then something like a boat.

It *was* a boat! With its sturdy lacquered hull, it floated beautifully.

Helping the townsfolk aboard, and making several trips back and forth, Paper John brought everyone safely to land.

When the town was rebuilt, the people wanted Paper John to be their mayor, but he said, "No, thank you. I prefer a simple life."

And so he continued to live in a paper house, and to make boats for the children, just as he had before.

As for the devil, his own trick turned against him. While the winds were destroying the town, he watched from the shore, laughing and dancing a jig. But the winds turned around and blew him away, too, all the way back to where he came from.